WITHDRAWN

SECRET CODERS
Robots & Repeats

GENE LUEN YANG & MIKE HOLMES

:01
First Second
New York

"It was this wonderful time between magic and so-called rationality."
–Wally Feurzeig, co-creator of the Logo programming language, on the early days of Logo

First Second
New York

Copyright © 2017 by Humble Comics LLC

Published by First Second
First Second is an imprint of Roaring Brook Press,
a division of Holtzbrinck Publishing Holdings Limited Partnership
175 Fifth Avenue, New York, New York 10010

Library of Congress Control Number: 2016961545

Paperback ISBN: 978-1-62672-605-5
Hardcover ISBN: 978-1-62672-606-2

Our books may be purchased in bulk for promotional, educational,
or business use. Please contact your local bookseller or the Macmillan Corporate
and Premium Sales Department at (800) 221-7945 ext. 5442 or by e-mail at
MacmillanSpecialMarkets@macmillan.com.

First edition 2017

Book design by Rob Steen

Printed in China by Toppan Leefung Printing Ltd., Dongguan City, Guangdong Province

Paperback: 10 9 8 7 6 5 4 3 2 1
Hardcover: 10 9 8 7 6 5 4 3 2 1

Chapter

4

I've been hiding here ever since, waiting for you.

So what I saw that night in the underground classroom...that wasn't my imagination after all!

Wait. You don't actually have a nose?

Where I'm from, noses are rather *rare*.

And where is that, exactly?

Australia!

Such a dummy.

All in due time, children, but first things first. You must learn to use the *Turtle of Light!* It's the only way to stop *Dr. One-Zero!*

As a demonstration, I would like you to try giving it some code.

?

Repeat 6 [
    Forward 15
    Left 60
]

9

Hey! This is almost exactly like *OpenSesame!* It's going to move forward fifteen steps...

Repeat 6 [
    Forward 15
    Left 60
]

Then turn left 60 degrees...

Repeat 6 [
    Forward 15
    Left 60
]

...and repeat five more times!

10

Ow.

My butt.

I'm sorry about that, Josh. I should've been more careful with my commands.

If you'd listened to me and gotten off of there, your *butt* wouldn't have gotten hurt.

Where did you get something like this, Professor Bee?

I brought it with me when I came to this dimen--

GRROWLL

Good thinking, Hopper.

But Cuddles is a lot sturdier than *Josh's butt.*

Will you guys *please* stop talking about my butt?!

We'll have to get him to go higher.

Yeah. Higher than *Josh's butt.*

GROWWLL

Let's hurry.

I got this, guys!

?

Not to brag or anything, but I'm pretty proud of the code I came up with. Right off the top of my head, you know?

It's some Eni-level stuff, so take your time to think it through.

Repeat 5 [
Forward 5
Right 90
Forward 5
Left 90
]

See if you can figure out what I made the Turtle of Light do.

Chapter

Did you figure it out? What do you think the Turtle of Light is gonna draw?

Good kitty, kitty...

Repeat 5 [
  Forward 5
  Right 90
  Forward 5
  Left 90
]

Repeat 5 [
    Forward 5
    Right 90
    Forward 5
    Left 90
]

Repeat 5 [
    Forward 5
    Right 90
    Forward 5
    Left 90
]

Repeat 5 [
    Forward 5
    Right 90
    Forward 5
    Left 90
]

CLEAR!

KRUNCH

Woohoo! ClearScreen rules!

Professor Bee! You're okay! Again!

Thanks to you all! My goodness, you've become such *accomplished coders!*

CODERS 1000

But not accomplished *enough*.

Professor Bee! I thought we were having a *moment* here!

Hopper, you said the same code twice. You could have used a Repeat instead.

But I *did* use a Repeat!

Yes, but you can use *more* than one in the same code, and you can *nest* them. Allow me to demonstrate.

Nest? Like a *bird?* We're dealing with *turtles* here, Professor!

?

EdAll

I'm typing in Hopper's code and giving it the name *Staircase*.

```
To Staircase
Repeat 5 [
Forward 5
Right 90
Forward 5
Left 90
]
End
```

The Turtle of Light has its own keyboard?

Keyboard of Light!

Give it a try.

?

Staircase

Do you see now? We've arrived at the same *result*, but the code is much more *elegant*.

What are you doing, Eni?

I'm changing it so that the outer Repeat runs *four* times instead of *two*.

ClearScreen

?

Staircase

Can we talk for a moment, dear?

Sure, Mom.

I heard from a little birdie that on the very first day of school, another student *spat* on you!

You mean *three* "little birdies."

And I heard the spitter is that *Hopper* girl you've been hanging out with so much! Is that true?

...

It's true.

Eni, spitting is *not* something we Wessons *tolerate!* You have to respect yourself enough to--

Hopper didn't start it, Mom. I threw a spoonful of pudding at her first. *On purpose.*

Eni Charles Wesson! Why in the *world* would you do a thing like *that?!*

I don't know. I just did.

You are to *stay away* from that young lady! You hear me?!

Mom--

If you want to play college ball, you've got to *focus* right now! You can't let all these *bad influences* distract you!

Hopper isn't *bad*, Mom.

That came out wrong, dear.

Listen. Sometimes two individuals can be *perfectly fine* on their own, but when they're together, they bring out the *worst* in each other.

You have to trust me on this.

No more hanging out with Hopper. Understood?

Yes, ma'am.

Hey, guys.

What's up?

What's this assembly all about, you think?

I don't know.

Hey, look, Eni! Your sisters! I think one of them might have a crush on me!

Um, no.

Put your hand down, Josh. I don't want them to know I'm with you guys.

How come?

Long story. I don't want to talk about it.

Hey! That's my line!

Good morning, Stately Academy! I've brought us together for one quick announcement!

Starting today, all your classes will be shortened by half in order to make room for a brand-new class: *Advanced Chemistry!*

What?!

He can't do that!

I will be teaching Advanced Chemistry *myself*, and it will be *required* for every Stately Academy student!

Thank you for your attention! You are dismissed!

Chemistry?

I know, right? Why chemistry?

We got our answer that afternoon.

Next, we're supposed to add a pinch of the white powder.

Wait. That looks like--

--Green Pop!

So that's his game.

He's turning the whole school into a *Green Pop—making factory!*

Pass me that cork, Eni.

You're stealing Green Pop? Why?

So I can--

Hey, guys! I want you to meet my lab partner, *Paz!*

Hello.

Nice to meet you, Paz.

Paz and I were just, you know, getting to know each other and...

Paz, why don't you tell them what you told me?

Hopper, I've been thinking.

Things have gotten awfully weird at *Stately Academy*. You've never felt comfortable there. Maybe it's time to move on.

No, Mom!

Eni, Josh, and I are the only ones who know how *evil* Principal One-Zero is! It's up to us to *stop* him!

But that's what the *police* are for, honey.

The police won't believe us! They think the campus was attacked by an unmanned drone! Don't tell me *you* don't believe us, either, Mom!

Of course I believe you, Hopper. I just don't think it should be up to a group of *kids* to stop somebody like that.

Maybe it *shouldn't* be, but it *is.*

You still haven't told me why we're here.

I'm trying to keep a *promise.* I'll be right back.

UNIVERSITY HOSPITAL

Green?

Green?

Green?

Green?

Excuse me, Mister Doctor Sir? Are you in charge of this patient?

I'm one of the doctors studying-- I mean, *caring for* Mr. Dean, yes.

Well, have I got something for you! *This* is what's causing his condition!

This looks like *soda pop*.

It *is* soda pop! But if you drink it--

Young lady, we are all well aware of the dangers of soda pop. I assure you that they have nothing to do with the *virus* that's ailing Mr. Dean.

Virus?! It's not a *virus!* It's--

Please see your way out, young lady.

Josh!

KLANK

Hey! Is Paz with you? I told her to come check out my sky hook!

Nope. I'm sure she *hates* when people tell her to come check out their sky hooks.

Where's Eni?

He didn't show up for practice. I thought he was with you.

I bet I know where to find him. Come on.

See? I told you there's more to it.

I'm guessing the Path Portal will give us a way into the conference room.

Let's see if I'm right.

Little Guy!

We're gonna have to use *Repeats*.

We're gonna have to use *nested* Repeats!

We'll use one Repeat to do a "petal"...

...and then *nest* that inside *another* Repeat to do the entire *"flower"*!

Chapter

The *outer Repeat* is on its *first repetition*. So is the *inner Repeat*. Josh, put one finger up.

Like this?

```
To DefeatTheCreep
  Repeat 4 [
    Repeat 3 [
    Forward 15
    Right 90
    ]
  ]
End
```

```
To DefeatTheCreep
  Repeat 4 [
    Repeat 3 [
    Forward 15
    Right 90
    ]
  ]
End
```

The outer Repeat *stays* on its first repetition. It won't move on until the inner Repeat finishes drawing a *petal*. Josh, you keep counting.

Okay... so the inner Repeat goes to *Repetition Two*.

```
To DefeatTheCreep
  Repeat 4 [
    Repeat 3 [
    Forward 15
    Right 90
    ]
  ]
End
```

```
To DefeatTheCreep
  Repeat 4 [
    Repeat 3 [
    Forward 15
    Right 90
    ]
  ]
End
```

Looks good. Now, after the turtle finishes walking one petal--

--it does a *Left 180* so it's facing the right way to do the *next one!*

TO DEFEAT THE CREEP
REPEAT 4 [
REPEAT 3 [
FORWARD 15
RIGHT 90
]
LEFT 180
]
END

Hey Josh--

Already *done!* They don't call me *Captain Speedy* for nothing!

Nobody calls you *Captain Speedy.*

SHUT:

?

DefeatTheCreep

All right, Josh. Let's go again. *Outer Repetition One.*

Inner Repetition One.

```
To DefeatTheCreep
  Repeat 4 [
    Repeat 3 [
      Forward 15
      Right 90
    ]

    Left 180
  ]
End
```

```
To DefeatTheCreep
  Repeat 4 [
    Repeat 3 [
      Forward 15
      Right 90
    ]

    Left 180
  ]
End
```

Still on *outer One.*

Inner Two.

```
To DefeatTheCreep
  Repeat 4 [
    Repeat 3 [
      Forward 15
      Right 90
    ]

    Left 180
  ]
End
```

```
To DefeatTheCreep
  Repeat 4 [
    Repeat 3 [
      Forward 15
      Right 90
    ]

    Left 180
  ]
End
```

Outer One.

Inner Three.

```
To DefeatTheCreep
  Repeat 4 [
    Repeat 3 [
      Forward 15
      Right 90
    ]
    Left 180
  ]
End
```

```
To DefeatTheCreep
  Repeat 4 [
    Repeat 3 [
      Forward 15
      Right 90
    ]
    Left 180
  ]
End
```

The inner Repeat has finished all three of its repetitions, but Little Guy still has one more instruction to follow.

What do I do now?

Just wait.

Let's see if our fix worked!

```
To DefeatTheCreep
  Repeat 4 [
    Repeat 3 [
      Forward 15
      Right 90
    ]
    Left 180
  ]
End
```

Looks good, Hopper. The outer Repeat is now on Repetition Two.

And the inner Repeat is Repetition One.

```
To DefeatTheCreep
  Repeat 4 [
    Repeat 3 [
      Forward 15
      Right 90
    ]

    Left 180
  ]
End
```

```
To DefeatTheCreep
  Repeat 4 [
    Repeat 3 [
      Forward 15
      Right 90
    ]

    Left 180
  ]
End
```

Outer Two.

Inner Two.

```
To DefeatTheCreep
  Repeat 4 [
    Repeat 3 [
      Forward 15
      Right 90
    ]

    Left 180
  ]
End
```

```
To DefeatTheCreep
  Repeat 4 [
    Repeat 3 [
      Forward 15
      Right 90
    ]

    Left 180
  ]
End
```

Outer Two.

Inner Three.

```
To DefeatTheCreep
  Repeat 4 [
    Repeat 3 [
      Forward 15
      Right 90
    ]

    Left 180
  ]
End
```

```
To DefeatTheCreep
  Repeat 4 [
    Repeat 3 [
      Forward 15
      Right 90
    ]

    Left 180
  ]
End
```

Here's the part where I wait again?

Yep.

Little Guy did the second petal *perfectly!*

```
To DefeatTheCreep
  Repeat 4 [
    Repeat 3 [
      Forward 15
      Right 90
    ]

    Left 180
  ]
End
```

What's so creepy about a *conference room?*

But it's *One-Zero's* conference room!

There are probably... I don't know... *skeletons* or something hidden in here!

Skeletons with *cash,* if we're lucky!

We're on *that* again?

This must be the whiteboard Paz was talking about.

I had no idea about that *secret entrance* to my own conference room!

One-Zero!

That's *Principal* One-Zero to you!

Toni? Lisa? Ronda? What are you doing with *him?*

We're trying to protect your *future*, Eni-baby!

We knew you'd just ignore us if we tried to stop you ourselves!

Good thing the principal was still in his office this late at night!

Last night, your children were caught *breaking* *and entering* into this very conference room! For what sort of *mischief*, I can only guess.

Eni Charles Wesson! What were you thinking?!

This, of course, would normally be grounds for *expulsion*, but I am a *merciful man*.

Your children may continue their studies at Stately Academy--

--*as long as they never socialize with one another ever again!*

What?!

Very wise, Principal One-Zero! I agree one hundred percent!

Well, I *disagree!* These children have been *positive influences* on one another!

64

So *positive* that they've become *criminals*, Ms. Hu?!

It's not like that, Mom.

We ought to have more *trust* in our children, Mrs. Wesson!

Dad? Aren't you gonna say something?

Mm? Oh, yes. Whatever the principal thinks is best, let's go with that.

With all due respect, Principal One-Zero, you can't tell us who we *can* and *can't* hang out with!

Oh, but don't you see?

I just did.

65

That was the start of my *worst day* since coming to Stately Academy.

⇒Sigh.⇐

Things didn't get much better in Advanced Chemistry. I wasn't allowed to work with Eni anymore, so I got paired up with a *rugby player*.

A pinch of the white powder... and done!

You know, One-Zero might be a creep, but the guy is an *excellent teacher!*

I've gotten an A on every single assignment!

That's because every single assignment is *exactly the same!*

Hey, all I know is, I'm *super-good* at chemistry now!

What the--?!

Check this out! Me and the guys figured this out the other day!

What did you do?!

Something *awesome!*

Hopper?
You have visitors.

Coders!

Oh man,
I can't tell
you how much
I *missed*
you guys!

Me too,
Hopper.

Even you,
dummy!

All right, all right!
I don't want Paz to
hear about this and
get *jealous!*

Um, I really don't
think you have to worry
about that, Josh.

I'll go see
if we've got
any *fruit
cups.*

Let me
show you guys
something
first.

Remember this game board?

Yeah, but there are only *four* columns! Each of the binary numbers on the map have *eight* digits!

You can add columns to the left.

Notice that every column is *twice* as tall as the one before it, so the next one will have sixteen boxes, then thirty-two, and so on.

I'm gonna need a bigger piece of paper.

No, you don't. Instead of drawing the entire column, just write the number of boxes at the top.

Like this?

Yeah. *Exactly* like that.

128 64 32 16 8 4 2 1

You guys are doing that thing again, where you *talk* and *talk* and I get *confused*.

CODERS 1010

CODERS 1010

Binary is how computers store numbers. Each digit in a *binary number* corresponds to a *column* on the game board.

Huh?

Now let's add up the numbers for each filled column.

64 + 8 + 2...

...equals 74!

So then, 01001010 and 74 are the same thing?

Way to put it all together, Captain Speedy!

See? People *do* call me Captain Speedy!

I was being *sarcastic!*

Whatever. But that still doesn't tell us anything. What is *74* supposed to mean?

Let's do the rest of these binary numbers. We can each take one.

Can we get some more paper, Hopper?

Here's 01000001.

Easy! 64 + 1...

...equals 65!

74, 65, 73, 76.

I *still* don't get what all this is supposed to mean.

Like I said, I talked to my dad about this.

Binary isn't just used to store *numbers* inside a computer.

It's used to store everything, including *letters*.

To store a letter, the computer first converts it to a *number* using an encoding scheme called *ASCII*. The number then gets converted into *binary*.

To figure out what the binary says, we just have to do the *reverse*.

Say the whole thing again. Only this time, *make sense*.

I'll show you. We've already converted the binary into *numbers*. Now we just have to convert the numbers into *letters*.

Check out this chart my dad gave me.

Man, Eni. You've got the *biggest pockets* of anybody I know.

83

Fine.
As long as it's
not Josherella.

"Light-Light"?! But there's no "Josh" in it at all!

Exactly. Now let's get out of here before Professor Bee wakes up.

Hold on. Don't you guys think Professor Bee is gonna notice that Josherella--

Light-Light.

--that *Light-Light* is gone?

I've got an idea.

```
Left 90
Repeat 3 [
    Forward 10
    Right 120
]
Forward 2
Right 90
Forward 2
Left 90
Forward 6
Left 90
Forward 2
```

According to the map, this is the place.

QUARTER CITY

This doesn't look like a jail at all.

Well, whatever it is, it's *creepy*.

This way.

Ducks with teeth are so *not cute*.

We have to get to the other side!

Time for *Light-Light*.

Good thinking! How many steps do you think it'll take to get all the way across? One hundred, maybe?

About that.

We can make a bridge that's sort of like a *ladder*, only it goes across instead of up.

I can *picture* it, Eni! It'll be a bunch of squares, one after the other!

We can use *nested Repeats*.

Josh! Bringing your A game!

Okay, we're gonna pause once more.

Let's do this, Coders!

Can you come up with code that makes a ladder-like bridge out of squares?

Continued in

Pop & Parameters

Ready to start coding?

Visit www.secret-coders.com

Check out these other books
in the Secret Coders series!

**Secret Coders
Paths & Portals
Secrets & Sequences**

GREAT GRAPHIC NOVELS

From the *New York Times*–Bestselling Author
Gene Luen Yang

AVAILABLE SEPARATELY OR AS A BOXED SET!

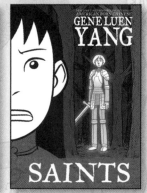

978-1-59643-152-2   978-1-59643-359-5   978-1-59643-689-3

"Gene Luen Yang has created that rare article: a youthful tale with something new to say about American youth."
—*The New York Times*

"Read this, and come away shaking."
—Gary Schmidt, Newbery Honor–winning author

"A masterful work of historical fiction."
—Dave Eggers, author of
A Heartbreaking Work of Staggering Genius

THE EXCITING NEW SERIES

978-1-62672-075-6

"Brings computer coding to life."
—*Entertainment Weekly*

978-1-59643-235-2

"Bravura storytelling."
—*Publishers Weekly*

978-1-59643-697-8

★ "A brilliant homage."
—*BCCB*

978-1-59643-156-0

★ "Absolutely not to be missed."
—*Booklist*

:01
First Second
NEW YORK